March 10, 2007

Dearest Alexander,

   Hope that you enjoy this mother Goose book as much as I delighted in picking it out for you with my friend and teacher, Ellen Peebles. I love you very much. Great grandma Janet

MOTHER GOOSE

LITTLE KITTY

MOTHER GOOSE

Illustrated by
Frederick Richardson

A Classic Collection
of Children's
Nursery Rhymes

This book was originally published in 1916.
First Dalmatian Press printing 2000.

MOTHER GOOSE
A Classic Collection of Children's Nursery Rhymes
Copyright © 2005 Dalmatian Press, LLC

The DALMATIAN PRESS name is a trademark
of Dalmatian Press, LLC, Franklin, Tennessee 37067.
No part of this book may be reproduced or copied in any form
without the written permission of Dalmatian Press.

ISBN: 1-40371-424-X
13916-0205

05 06 07 08 LPU 10 9 8 7 6 5 4 3 2 1

AN INTRODUCTION

by Yolanda D. Federici
Director of Children's Books Chicago Public Library

Mother Goose and the rhymes attributed to her are acknowledged favorites with children. Young children, even the littlest ones, show preferences in their choice of the sounds, words and books they want to hear read aloud. Before their hands can hold books, babies show an interest in the rhythmic lilt of Mother Goose rhymes. A three-month-old baby, for example, will listen with a wondering intentness to "Little Bo-Peep Has Lost Her Sheep." And "Bye, Baby Bunting," or "Hush-a-Bye, Baby," have a soothing rhythm that will lull a child to sleep. The many finger games and plays that identify parts of the body, like "This Little Piggy Went to Market," will bring many moments of delight. When the child has some control of his arms and hands, he will take part in, "Pat a Cake, Pat a Cake," and many of the other action rhymes. Later, the picture book itself will attract the child, and she will point to the colorful illustrations that accompany her favorite rhymes and demand that those be read.

As children grow, they learn the riddles and the ABC and counting rhymes. Then they want the longer ballads read aloud. There is actually something for everyone in Mother Goose. Even scholarly adults are intrigued by her possible origin, by the hidden meaning in the simple verses, and even which particular historical characters are being lampooned in them. Parents share with their children their own pleasant memories of hours of fun as children with such rhymes as "Hickory, Dickory, Dock," "Baa, Baa, Black Sheep," and all the other old friends in Mother Goose. Few books have the quality of appeal that lasts from one generation to another.

The longevity of this old lady and her offerings is probably due to the folk quality that is inherent in her origin as much as the lively nonsense, good commonsense, and variety in the verses. Some of the rhymes can be traced to popular ballads, folk songs and games, political satire, ancient proverbs, cries of street vendors, real or legendary events. These were known long before they were designated as Mother Goose rhymes. In fact, until the eighteenth century Mother Goose did not have a name in print in English literature.

Her name may have come from Charlemagne's mother who was known as Queen Goosefoot. *Mère l'Oye,* or Mother Goose, was well known in France for centuries as the supposed originator of any fabulous tale, particularly those for children.

Additions from old sources keep on increasing the number of pieces attributed to Mother Goose. These are taken from old proverbs, riddles, charms, and tongue-twisters. When adequate research is not done, familiar poems for children, whose authorship is declared anonymous, are frequently included. For example, "Twinkle, Twinkle Little Star" was written by Jane Taylor. Sara J. Hale wrote "Mary Had a Little Lamb," and Eliza Lee Follen wrote "The Three Little Kittens."

In every generation, distinguished authors and artists have felt the lure of doing their own Mother Goose collection. There is something about this folk character and her rhymes that stimulates imaginative people who remember her charm for young children, and who want to add their own interpretation. Mother Goose has worn many different costumes, but those that seem to suit her best are the ones currently worn as everyday clothing during the eighteenth century when she first acquired her name in print.

Her perennial attraction for children is the variety of interesting characters that troop through the pages of her books, and not all of the characters are good. "Little Boy Blue," for example, is asleep on the job. "Little Polly Flinders" is a careless little girl. And Simple Simon did his best to get something for nothing from the pieman. But Mother Goose is full of happy, busy children who are independent and ingenious. Another attraction is the natural contact that the child-characters have with the great grown-up world. The rhymes tell about festivals, vocations, courtship, marriage, and death. There are many adult characters in adult situations, like "Jack Sprat could eat no fat," "There was a crooked man," "Old woman, old woman, shall we go a-shearing?" "A Farmer went trotting upon his gray mare," and many others.

Friendly animals are everywhere, with cats and mice as special favorites, as in "I like little kitty; her coat is so warm," and "Hickory, dickory, dock! The mouse ran up the clock." Other rhymes are humorous and full of fantasy, such as "High diddle diddle/The cat and the fiddle" and "Three wise men from Gotham/Went to sea in a bowl." For older children, there is a more mature humor as in "The man in the wilderness/Asked me/How many strawberries/Grew in the sea." Action-filled and quickly resolved plots also charm the young and the older children: "The Queen of Hearts/She made some tarts," "Sing a song of sixpence," "Old King Cole," and so on. Then there are the riddles which seem at first glance incomprehensible yet always fascinate the young.

Here is the wealth of Mother Goose presented for the delight of children and adults of all ages. She is a very old lady who remains youthful and vigorous; and remarkably she is able to charm every new generation.

A FOREWORD

Children, as well as their interested parents, will eagerly welcome this beautiful edition of the one great nursery classic, just as a worthy edition of Shakespeare is welcomed by discriminating adult readers.

But some may ask what there is in these simple melodies, attributed to Mother Goose, which gives them so secure and beloved a place in the home, the school and the public library. Is it the humor, the action, the rhythm, or the mystery of the theme which appeals so strongly to critical little minds in each generation of childhood, and even to adult minds so fortunate as to have retained some of the refreshing naiveté of early years?

It is useless to try to explain the charm of these nonsense melodies. The children themselves do not know why they love them. No mother can tell us the magic of the spell which seems to be cast over her restless baby as she croons to it a Mother Goose lullaby. No primary teacher quite understands why the mere repetition or singing of a Mother Goose jingle will transform her listless, inattentive class into one all eagerness and attention. But mother and teacher agree that the best of these verses have an even more potent influence than that of innocently diverting and entertaining the child. The healthy moral, so subtly suggested in many of the rhymes, is unconsciously absorbed by the child's receptive mind, helping him to make his own distinction between right and wrong, bravery and cowardice, generosity and selfishness.

From a literary standpoint, also, these rhymes have proved of real value in creating a taste for the truly musical in poetry and song. They train the ear and stir the imagination of the child as no other verses do. Many famous poets and writers trace their first inspiration, and love for things literary, back to the nursery songs and fairy tales of their childhood.

Teachers well know that children who have reveled in these rhymes and stories, at the time of their strongest appeal, step naturally and appreciatively into the great fields of good literature which are beyond.

Knowing these things to be true, we do not hesitate to place this venerable classic on the shelf beside our Shakespeare, and to send our children there for delight and inspiration. They will understand Shakespeare the better for having known and loved Mother Goose.

But what about the personality of this classic writer? Was she really Mistress Elizabeth Goose who is said to have lived in Boston about two hundred years ago, and who crooned her nonsense jingles to a large and happy family of grandchildren? We are told that their father, Thomas Fleet, who was a printer by trade, thought to turn an honest penny with his mother-in-law's popular verses, so he published them in a small volume under the title of *Songs for the Nursery: or, Mother Goose's Melodies*. A goose with a very long neck and a wide-open mouth flew across the title page, at least so the story goes. But we have to believe that it is only a story, for no copy of the book can be found, and nothing but tradition identifies Elizabeth Goose, the Boston grandmother, with the famous rhymester.

We might feel sorry to be obliged to discredit this picturesque story of Mother Goose, if her real history were not even more mysterious. We know very little about the beloved patron of childhood, but what we do know is as follows:

Mother Goose is most certainly of respectable French origin, for in 1697 a distinguished French writer, Charles Perrault, published in Paris a little book of familiar stories called *Contes de ma Mère l'Oye*, or "Tales of My Mother Goose." Her identity, however, he leaves a mystery, except that in the frontispiece of his book is pictured an old woman by her fireside telling stories to an eager little family group.

This volume contained the only prose tales that have ever been credited to Mother Goose, and they are still among the most popular stories in nursery or school room. The titles are as follows: "Little Red Riding Hood"; "The Sisters Who Dropped from Their Mouths Diamonds and Toads"; "Bluebeard"; "The Sleeping Beauty"; "Puss in Boots"; "Cinderella"; "Riquet with the Tuft"; and "Tom Thumb."

It is through her verses, however, that Mother Goose has won her well-deserved fame. The first collection under her name was published in London about 1765 by John Newbery. It may be, if Oliver Goldsmith were living, he could tell us more about the origin of these verses than we are now ever likely to know. It is more than probable that he himself edited the little volume for John Newbery, and that he wrote the clever preface, "By a very Great Writer of very Little Books," as well as the quaint moral which supplements each rhyme.

About twenty-five years later this book was reprinted in our country by Isaiah Thomas of Worcester, Massachusetts. Several copies of this edition are preserved, one of which has been photographed and reproduced in facsimile by W. H. Whitmore of Boston. Other publishers also reprinted the English edition, one being done for John Newbery's grandson, Francis Power, in 1791.

In 1810 another collection of melodies appeared under the title of *Gammer Gurton's Garland*. It was quite evidently a rival of Mother Goose, though it contained nearly all of her verses, besides many far less interesting ones gathered from other sources.

Gammer Gurton's popularity, however, was short, and Mother Goose was revived about 1825 by a Boston firm, Munroe and Francis. Since that time her fame has never waned. In spite of the present multiplicity of beautiful books for children, they are constantly exhausting large editions of the one universally beloved book of melodies. Some of these volumes have been

collected and edited by men of the highest literary judgment and ability, such as Goldsmith (with hardly a doubt), Ritson, Halliwell, Andrew Lang, Charles Eliot Norton, Charles Welsh and Edward Everett Hale. Certainly there is not another collection of juvenile literature which can boast such a list of scholarly editors. The deepest gratitude is due them for their careful and discriminating effort to preserve for the children of future generations this rich heritage of nursery melodies.

Many less discriminating editors, however, have ruthlessly mutilated and adapted many of the rhymes to suit their fancy, thinking, possibly, that as Mother Goose is only a title, the verses attributed to her belong to the general public to use as it sees fit. On the contrary, Mother Goose's melodies belong to the children, and no addition or change should be made except by those who are in such close sympathy with the childheart that they may act with the child's authority.

This present edition of *Mother Goose* preserves the best of the verses which became so popular in England and America as to first demand their publication. It is the only truly classic edition that has been published in modern times. The two authorities which have been followed are the edition published for John Newbery's grandson in London in 1791, and probably edited by Oliver Goldsmith, and the edition published in Boston in 1833 by Munroe and Francis, called *The Only True Mother Goose Melodies*. It is from this copy that the quaint introduction by "Ma'am Goose" is quoted.

Not all the favorites among the nursery rhymes are here, only those that first helped to make the fame of the fictitious but no less worthy patron of childhood. May her fame and her melodies be lovingly preserved to give joy and inspiration to many future generations of little children.

EULALIE OSGOOD GROVER

From "The Only True Mother Goose Melodies"
Published by Munroe & Francis, Boston 1833

TABLE OF CONTENTS

(For an alphabetical list of first lines, see pp. 113–117.)

TABLE OF CONTENTS—*Continued*

2

TABLE OF CONTENTS—*Continued*

PAT A CAKE

Hear what
ma'am goose says!

My dear little Blossoms, there are now in this world, and always will be, a great many grannies besides myself, both in petticoats and pantaloons, some a deal younger, to be sure, but all monstrous wise and of my own family name. These old women, who never had chick or child of their own, but who always know how to bring up other people's children, will tell you with long faces that my enchanting, quieting, soothing volume, my all-sufficient anodyne for cross, peevish, won't-be-comforted little children, ought be laid aside for more learned books, such as *they* could select and publish.

Nonsense! I tell you all their batterings can't deface my beauties nor their wise pratings equal my wiser prattlings; and all imitators of my refreshing songs might as well write another Billy Shakespeare as another Mother Goose—we two great poets were born together, and shall go out of the world together.

No, no, my melodies will never die,
While nurses sing, or babies cry.

Old Mother Goose

Old Mother Goose, when
　　She wanted to wander,
Would ride through the air
　　On a very fine gander.

Mother Goose had a house,
　　'Twas built in a wood.
An owl at the door
　　For a porter stood.

She had a son Jack,
　　A plain-looking lad.
He was not very good,
　　Nor yet very bad.

She sent him to market,
　　A live goose he bought.
"Here! mother," says he,
　　"It will not go for naught."

Jack's goose and her gander
　　Grew very fond;
They'd both eat together,
　　Or swim in one pond.

Jack found one morning,
　　As I have been told,
His goose had laid him
　　An egg of pure gold.

Jack rode to his mother,
　　The news for to tell.
She called him a good boy
　　And said it was well.

And Old Mother Goose
　　The goose saddled soon,
And mounting its back,
　　Flew up to the moon.

OLD MOTHER GOOSE

COCK-A-DOODLE-DOO

Cock-a-doodle-doo,
My dame has lost her shoe.
My master's lost his fiddlestick,
And knows not what to do.

THE PUMPKIN EATER

Peter, Peter, pumpkin eater,
Had a wife and couldn't keep her;
He put her in a pumpkin shell,
    And then he kept her very well.

Peter, Peter, pumpkin eater,
Had another and didn't love her;
Peter learned to read and spell,
    And then he loved her very well.

THE HOBBY HORSE

I had a little hobby horse,
    And it was dapple gray.
Its head was made of pea-straw,
    Its tail was made of hay.
I sold it to an old woman
    For a copper groat;
And I'll not sing my song again
    Without another coat.

A WEEK OF BIRTHDAYS

Monday's child is fair of face,
Tuesday's child is full of grace,
Wednesday's child is full of woe,
Thursday's child has far to go,
Friday's child is loving and giving,
Saturday's child works hard for
        a living;
But the child that is born on the
        Sabbath day
Is bonny and blithe and good and gay.

ONE MISTY MOISTY MORNING

One misty, moisty morning,
  When cloudy was the weather,
I chanced to meet an old man
    clothed all in leather.
He began to compliment,
    and I began to grin,
How do you do, and how do you do?
And how do you do again?

MARY HAD A LITTLE LAMB

Mary had a little lamb
With fleece as white as snow.
And everywhere that Mary went
The lamb was sure to go.

It followed her to school one day—
That was against the rule.
It made the children laugh and play
To see a lamb at school.

And so the teacher turned it out,
But still it lingered near,
And waited patiently about
Till Mary did appear.

"Why does the lamb love Mary so?"
The eager children cry.
"Why, Mary loves the lamb,
    you know!"
The teacher did reply.

LITTLE KITTY

I like little kitty, her coat is so warm.
And if I don't hurt her she'll do me
    no harm.
So I'll not pull her tail, nor drive her
    away,
But kitty and I very gently will play.

A CANDLE

Little Nanny Etticoat
In a white petticoat,
And a red nose;
The longer she stands
The shorter she grows.

A·B·C·D·E·F·G

A, B, C, D, E, F, G,
H, I, J, K, L, M, N, O, P,
Q, R, S and T, U, V,
W, X and Y and Z.
Now I've said my A B C,
Tell me what you think of me.

GOOD ADVICE

Come when you're called,
  Do what you're bid,
Shut the door after you,
  And never be chid.

THE MAN IN THE WILDERNESS

The man in the wilderness
  Asked me
How many strawberries
  Grew in the sea.
I answered him
  As I thought good,
As many red herrings
  As grew in the wood.

BIRDS OF A FEATHER

Birds of a feather flock together,
And so will pigs and swine.
Rats and mice have their choice,
And so will I have mine.

BILLY, BILLY

"Billy, Billy, come and play,
While the sun shines bright as day."

"Yes, my Polly, so I will,
For I love to please you still."

"Billy, Billy, have you seen
Sam and Betsy on the green?"

"Yes, my Poll, I saw them pass,
Skipping o'er the new-mown grass."

FEARS AND TEARS

Tommy's tears and Mary's fears
Will make them old before their years.

LITTLE BO-PEEP

LITTLE BO-PEEP

Little Bo-Peep has lost her sheep,
And can't tell where to find them.
Leave them alone,
    and they'll come home,
And bring their tails
    behind them.

Little Bo-Peep fell fast asleep,
And dreamt she heard them
    bleating;
But when she awoke she found
    it a joke,
For still they all were fleeting.

Then up she took her little crook,
Determined for to find them.
She found them indeed,
    but it made her heart bleed,
For they'd left all their tails
    behind 'em!

It happened one day, as Bo-Peep
    did stray
Unto a meadow hard by—
There she espied their tails,
    side by side,
All hung on a tree to dry.

She heaved a sigh and wiped
    her eye,
And over the hillocks she raced;
And tried what she could,
    as a shepherdess should,
That each tail should be
    properly placed.

GO TO BED FIRST

Go to bed first,
A golden purse;
Go to bed second,
A golden pheasant;
Go to bed third,
A golden bird.

DREAMS

Friday night's dream,
    on Saturday told,
Is sure to come true,
    be it never so old.

SHOEING

Shoe the colt,
Shoe the colt,
Shoe the wild mare;
Here a nail,
There a nail,
Colt must go bare.

RIDE AWAY, RIDE AWAY

Ride away, ride away,
    Johnny shall ride,
And he shall have pussy-cat
    Tied to one side.
And he shall have little dog
    Tied to the other,
And Johnny shall ride
    To see his grandmother.

TOMMY TITTLEMOUSE

Little Tommy Tittlemouse
Lived in a little house.
He caught fishes
In other men's ditches.

HUSH-A-BYE

Hush-a-bye, Baby, upon the tree top,
When the wind blows the cradle will rock;
When the bough breaks the cradle will fall,
Down tumbles cradle and Baby and all.

THE CLOCK

There's a neat little clock—
   In the schoolroom it stands—
And it points to the time
   With its two little hands.

And may we, like the clock,
   Keep a face clean and bright,
With hands ever ready
   To do what is right.

ABOUT THE BUSH

About the bush, Willie, about the
     bee-hive,
About the bush, Willie, I'll meet thee
     alive.

MY MOTHER SAID

My mother said that I never should
Play with the gypsies in the wood.
The wood was dark, the grass
     was green;
By came Sally with a tambourine.
I went to sea—no ship to get across;
I paid ten shillings for a blind
     white horse.
I upped on his back and was off
     in a crack,
Sally, tell my mother I shall never
     come back.

A cat came fiddling

A cat came fiddling out of a barn,
With a pair of bagpipes under
    her arm.
She could sing nothing but,
    "Fiddle-de-dee,
The mouse has married the
    bumble-bee."
Pipe, cat!
Dance, mouse!
We'll have a wedding at our
    good house.

If wishes were horses

If wishes were horses,
    Beggars would ride.
If turnips were watches,
    I would wear one by my side.
And if "ifs" and "ands"
    Were pots and pans
There'd be no work for tinkers!

Betty blue

    Little Betty Blue
    Lost her holiday shoe.
What will poor Betty do?
    Why, give her another
    To match the other,
And then she will walk in two.

The black hen

Hickety, pickety, my black hen,
She lays eggs for gentlemen.
Gentlemen come every day
To see what my black hen doth lay.

MARY MOREY

I'll tell you a story
About Mary Morey,
And now my story's begun.
I'll tell you another
About her brother,
And now my story's done.

WHEN THE SNOW
IS ON THE GROUND

The little robin grieves
When the snow is on the ground,
For the trees have no leaves,
And no berries can be found.

The air is cold, the worms are hid;
For robin here what can be done?
Let's strow around some crumbs of bread,
And then he'll live till snow is gone.

WHEN THE SNOW IS ON THE GROUND

HICKORY, DICKORY, DOCK

Hickory, dickory, dock,
The mouse ran up the clock.
The clock struck one,
The mouse ran down,
Hickory, dickory, dock.

THREE LITTLE KITTENS

Three little kittens lost their
    mittens,
    And they began to cry,
    "Oh! mother dear, we very much
    fear
That we have lost our mittens."
"Lost your mittens! You naughty
    kittens!
    Then you shall have have no pie."
      Mee-ow, mee-ow, mee-ow.
    "No, you shall have no pie."
      Mee-ow, mee-ow, mee-ow.

The three little kittens found their
    mittens
    And they began to cry,
    "Oh! mother dear, see here,
    see here,
See, we have found our mittens."
"Put on your mittens, you silly
    kittens,
    And you may have some pie."
      Purr-r, purr-r, purr-r.
    "Oh! let us have the pie."
      Purr-r, purr-r, purr-r.

The three little kittens put on their
    mittens,
    And soon ate up the pie.
    "Oh! mother dear, we greatly
    fear
That we have soiled our mittens."
"Soiled your mittens! You naughty
    kittens!"
    Then they began to sigh,
      Mee-ow, mee-ow, mee-ow.
    Then they began to sigh,
      Mee-ow, mee-ow, mee-ow.

The three little kittens washed their
    mittens
    And hung them out to dry.
    "Oh! mother dear, do you not hear,
    That we have washed our
    mittens?"
"Washed your mittens! Oh! you're
    good kittens,
    But I smell a rat close by."
      Hush! hush! Mee-ow, mee-ow.
    "We smell a rat close by."
      Mee-ow, mee-ow, mee-ow.

THREE YOUNG RATS

Three young rats with black felt hats,
Three young ducks with white
    straw flats,
Three young dogs with curling tails,
Three young cats with demi-veils,
Went out to walk with three
    young pigs
In satin vests and sorrel wigs.
But suddenly it chanced to rain
And so they all went home again.

SEE-SAW, SACRADOWN

See-saw, sacradown,
Which is the way to London town?
One foot up, the other foot down,
That is the way to London town.

THE MIST

A hill full, a hole full,
Yet you cannot catch a bowl full.

WEE WILLIE WINKIE

Wee Willie Winkie runs through
    the town,
Upstairs and downstairs, in his
    nightgown,
Tapping at the window, crying
    at the lock,
"Are the babes in their beds?—
    for now it's eight o'clock!"

JACK

Jack, be nimble! Jack, be quick!
Jack, jump over the candlestick!

Baa, baa, black sheep

Baa, baa, black sheep,
Have you any wool?
Yes, marry, have I,
Three bags full:
One for my master,
One for my dame,
And one for the little boy
Who cries in the lane.

THE MAN WHO
HAD NAUGHT

There was a man and he had naught,
　And robbers came to rob him.
He crept up to the chimney top,
　And then they thought they had him.

But he got down on the other side,
　And then they could not find him.
He ran fourteen miles in fifteen days,
　And never looked back behind him.

TWEEDLE-DUM
AND TWEEDLE-DEE

Tweedle-dum and Tweedle-dee
　Resolved to have a battle,
For Tweedle-dum said Tweedle-dee
　Had spoiled his nice new rattle.

Just then flew by a monstrous crow,
　As big as a tar barrel,
Which frightened both the heroes so,
　They quite forgot their quarrel.

BOBBY SHAFTOE

Bobby Shaftoe's gone to sea,
With silver buckles on his knee.
He'll come back to marry me,
　　Pretty Bobby Shaftoe.

Bobby Shaftoe's fat and fair,
Combing down his yellow hair.
He's my love forevermore,
　　Pretty Bobby Shaftoe.

SING A SONG OF SIXPENCE

Sing a Song of Sixpence

Sing a song of sixpence,
A pocket full of rye,
Four and twenty blackbirds
Baked in a pie.

When the pie was opened
The birds began to sing,
And wasn't this a dainty dish
To set before the king?

The king was in the parlor
Counting out his money;
The queen was in the kitchen
Eating bread and honey;

The maid was in the garden
Hanging out the clothes,
There came a little blackbird
And nipped off her nose.

WILLIE BOY

Willie boy, Willie boy,
　　Where are you going?
O, let us go with you
　　This sunshiny day.

I'm going to the meadow
　　To see them a-mowing,
I'm going to help the girls
　　Turn the new hay.

TEETH AND GUMS

Thirty white horses upon a red hill,
Now they tramp, now they champ,
　　Now they stand still.

THERE WAS A LADY LOVED A SWINE

There was a lady loved a swine.
　　"Honey," quoth she,
"Pig-hog, wilt thou be mine?"
　　"Hoogh," quoth he.

"I'll build thee a silver sty,
　　Honey," quoth she,
"And in it thou shalt lie."
　　"Hoogh," quoth he.

"Pinned with a silver pin,
　　Honey," quoth she,
"That thou may go out and in."
　　"Hoogh," quoth he.

"Wilt thou have me now,
　　Honey?" quoth she.
"Speak or my heart will break."
　　"Hoogh," quoth he.

THREE WISE MEN OF GOTHAM

Three wise men of Gotham
Went to sea in a bowl.
If the bowl had been stronger
My song would be longer.

TO MARKET

To market, to market, to buy a fat pig,
Home again, home again, jiggety jig.

THREE CHILDREN ON THE ICE

Three children sliding on the ice
   Upon a summer's day,
As it fell out, they all fell in,
   The rest they ran away.

Oh, had these children been at school,
   Or sliding on dry ground,
Ten thousand pounds to one penny
   They had not then been drowned.

Ye parents who have children dear,
   And ye, too, who have none,
If you would keep them safe abroad,
   Pray keep them safe at home.

PETER PIPER

Peter Piper picked a peck
      of pickled peppers;
A peck of pickled peppers
      Peter Piper picked.
If Peter Piper picked a peck
      of pickled peppers,
Where's the peck of pickled
      peppers Peter Piper picked?

BETTY BOTTER

Betty Botter bought some butter,
   But she said, the butter's bitter.
If I put it in my batter,
   It will make my batter bitter;
But a bit of better butter,
   That would make my batter better.
So she bought a bit of butter
   Better than her bitter butter,
And she put it in her batter
   And the batter was not bitter.
So 'twas better Betty Botter
   Bought a bit of better butter.

HIE TO THE MARKET

Hie* to the market, Jenny come trot,
Spilt all her buttermilk, every drop!
   Every drop and every dram—
Jenny came home
   with an empty can.

* hie—hurry

35

THE BOUGHS DO SHAKE

The boughs do shake and the
    bells do ring,
So merrily comes our harvest in,
Our harvest in, our harvest in,
So merrily comes our harvest in.

We've plowed, we've sowed,
We've reaped, we've mowed,
We've got our harvest in.

IF ALL THE SEAS WERE ONE SEA

If all the seas were one sea,
What a *great* sea that would be!
And if all the trees were one tree,
What a *great* tree that would be!
And if all the axes were one axe,
What a *great* axe that would be!
And if all the men were one man,
What a *great* man he would be!
And if the *great* man took
    the *great* axe,
And cut down the *great* tree,
And let it fall into the *great* sea,
What a splish splash *that* would be!

CÆSAR'S SONG

Bow, wow, wow!
  Whose dog art thou?
  Little Tom Tinker's dog,
Bow, wow, wow!

BARBER, BARBER

Barber, barber, shave a pig.
How many hairs will make a wig?
Four and twenty; that's enough.
Give the barber a pinch of snuff.

LITTLE JUMPING JOAN

Here am I, little jumping Joan.
When nobody's with me
I'm always alone.

SIMPLE SIMON

Simple Simon met a pieman
　　Going to the fair.
Says Simple Simon to the pieman:
　　"Pray let me taste your ware."

Says the pieman to Simple Simon:
　　"Show me first your penny."
Says Simple Simon to the pieman:
　　"Indeed I have not any."

Simple Simon went a-fishing
　　For to catch a whale.
All the water he could find
　　Was in his mother's pail!

Simple Simon went to look
　　If plums grew on a thistle.
He pricked his fingers very much,
　　Which made poor Simon whistle.

He went to catch a dicky bird,
　　And thought he could not fail,
Because he had a little salt
　　To put upon its tail.

He went for water with a sieve,
　　But soon it ran all through.
And now poor Simple Simon
　　Bids you all adieu.

SIMPLE SIMON

LITTLE MISS MUFFET

Little Miss Muffet
Sat on a tuffet
Eating some curds and whey.
There came a great spider,
That sat down beside her,
And frightened Miss Muffet away.

WHISTLE

"Whistle, daughter, whistle;
    Whistle, daughter dear."
"I cannot whistle, mommy,
    I cannot whistle clear."
"Whistle, daughter, whistle;
    Whistle for a pound."
"I cannot whistle, mommy,
    I cannot make a sound."

AN ICICLE

Lives in winter, dies in summer,
And grows with its roots upward!

GEORGY PORGY

Georgy Porgy, pudding and pie,
Kissed the girls and made them cry.
When the boys came out to play,
Georgy Porgy ran away.

OLD WOMAN

There was an old woman
    lived under the hill,
And if she's not gone
    she lives there still.

Baked apples she sold
    and cranberry pies,
And she's the old woman
    that never told lies.

TOM, TOM, THE PIPER'S SON

Tom, Tom, the piper's son,
Stole a pig, and away he run.
    The pig was eat,
    And Tom was beat,
And Tom ran crying down the street.

ROBIN HOOD

Robin Hood, Robin Hood,
    Is in the mickle wood!
Little John, Little John,
    He to the town is gone.

Robin Hood, Robin Hood,
    Telling his beads,*
All in the greenwood
    Among the green weeds.

Little John, Little John,
    If he comes no more,
Robin Hood, Robin Hood,
    We shall fret full sore!

* praying with his rosary beads
† kirk—church

THE GIRL AND THE BIRDS

When I was a little girl,
About seven years old,
I hadn't got a petticoat,
To cover me from the cold.

So I went into Darlington,
That pretty little town,
And there I bought a petticoat,
A cloak, and a gown.

I went into the woods
And built me a kirk.†
And all the birds of the air,
They helped me to work.

The hawk with his long claws
Pulled down the stone,
The dove with her rough bill
Brought me them home.

The parrot was the clergyman,
The peacock was the clerk,
The bullfinch played the organ;
We made merry work.

BYE, BABY BUNTING

Bye, Baby bunting,
Father's gone a-hunting,
Mother's gone a-milking,
Sister's gone a-silking,
And Brother's gone to buy a skin
To wrap the Baby bunting in.

JACK AND JILL

Jack and Jill went up the hill
To fetch a pail of water.
Jack fell down and broke his crown,
And Jill came tumbling after.

BLIND MAN

Blind man, blind man,
 Sure you can't see?
Turn round three times,
 And try to catch me.
Turn east, turn west,
 Catch as you can,
Did you think you'd caught me?
 Blind, blind man!

SIR SIMON

Old Sir Simon the king,
And young Sir Simon the squire,
And old Mrs. Hickabout
Kicked Mrs. Kickabout
Round about our coal fire.

RED STOCKINGS

Red stockings, blue stockings,
 Shoes tied up with silver.
A red rosette upon my breast
 And a gold ring on my finger.

THERE WAS AN OLD MAN

There was an old man,
 And he had a calf,
 And that's half.
He took him out of the stall,
 And put him on the wall,
 And that's all.

THE BELLS

THE BELLS

"You owe me five shillings,"
Say the bells of St. Helen's.

"When will you pay me?"
Say the bells of Old Bailey.

"When I grow rich,"
Say the bells of Shoreditch.

"When will that be?"
Say the bells of Stepney.

"I do not know,"
Says the great Bell of Bow.

"Two sticks in an apple,"
Ring the bells of Whitechapel.

"Halfpence and farthings,"
Say the bells of St. Martin's.

"Kettles and pans,"
Say the bells of St. Ann's.

"Brickbats and tiles,"
Say the bells of St. Giles.

"Old shoes and slippers,"
Say the bells of St. Peter's.

"Pokers and tongs,"
Say the bells of St. John's.

A WISE OLD OWL

A wise old owl sat in an oak.
The more he heard the less he spoke;
The less he spoke the more he heard.
Why aren't we all like that
　　　wise old bird?

ELSIE MARLEY

Elsie Marley is grown so fine,
She won't get up to feed the swine,
But lies in bed till eight or nine.
　　　Lazy Elsie Marley.

RING A RING
o' ROSES

Ring a ring o' roses,
A pocket full of posies.
Tisha! Tisha!
We all fall down.

PUSSYCAT AND
THE QUEEN

Pussy cat, pussy cat,
　　　where have you been?
I've been to London
　　　to see the Queen.
Pussy cat, pussy cat,
　　　what did you there?
I frightened a little mouse
　　　under the chair.

A WALNUT

As soft as silk, as white as milk,
As bitter as gall, a strong wall,
　　　And a green coat covers me all.

PAT A CAKE

Pat a cake, pat a cake, Baker's man;
Make me a cake as fast as you can.
Pat it and prick it and mark it with B,
Put it in the oven for Baby and me.

LITTLE BOY BLUE

Little Boy Blue, come blow your horn,
The sheep's in the meadow, the cow's in the corn.
What! Is this the way you mind your sheep,
Under the haystack fast asleep?

DEAR, DEAR!

Dear, dear! What can the matter be?
Two old women got up in an apple tree.
One came down, and the other
    stayed till Saturday.

LITTLE POLLY FLINDERS

Little Polly Flinders
Sat among the cinders
   Warming her pretty toes.
Her mother came and caught her,
Spanked her little daughter
   For spoiling her nice new clothes.

PUSSY-CAT ATE THE DUMPLINGS

Pussy-cat ate the dumplings,
    the dumplings,
   Pussy-cat ate the dumplings.
Mamma stood by, and cried,
    "Oh, fie!
Why did you eat the dumplings?"

MARY'S CANARY

Mary had a pretty bird,
   Feathers bright and yellow,
Slender legs—upon my word
   He was a pretty fellow!

The sweetest note he always sung,
   Which much delighted Mary.
She often, where the cage was hung,
   Sat hearing her canary.

BOY AND GIRL

There was a little boy and a little girl
   Lived in an alley.
Says the little boy to the little girl,
   "Shall I, oh, shall I?"

Says the little girl to the little boy,
   "What shall we do?"
Says the little boy to the little girl,
   "I will kiss you."

JERRY HALL

Jerry Hall, he was so small,
A rat could eat him, hat and all.

THE CLEVER HEN

I had a little hen, the prettiest
   ever seen.
  She washed me the dishes
   and kept the house clean.
  She went to the mill to fetch me
   some flour,
And always got home
   in less than an hour.
  She baked me my bread,
   she brewed me my ale,
  She sat by the fire and told
   many a fine tale.

CACKLE, CACKLE

Cackle, cackle, Mother Goose,
   Have you any feathers loose?
Truly have I, pretty fellow,
   Half enough to fill a pillow.
Here are quills, take one or two,
   And down to make a bed for you.

THE MAN IN THE MOON

The man in the moon came down too soon
To inquire the way to Norridge.
The man in the south, he burnt his mouth
With eating cold plum porridge.

OLD WOMAN, OLD WOMAN

There was an old woman tossed up in a basket
Seventeen times as high as the moon;
But where she was going no mortal could tell,
For under her arm she carried a broom.

"Old woman, old woman, old woman," said I,
"Whither, oh whither, oh whither so high?"
"To sweep the cobwebs from the sky,
And I'll be with you by and by."

OLD WOMAN, OLD WOMAN

LITTLE JACK HORNER

Little Jack Horner
Sat in a corner,
Eating a Christmas pie.
He put in his thumb,
And pulled out a plum,
And said: "Oh, what a good boy am I!"

SWAN, SWAN

Swan, swan, over the sea.
Swim, swan, swim!
Swan, swan, back again.
Well swum, swan!

THE GREEDY MAN

The greedy man is he who sits
    And bites bits out of plates,
Or else takes up an almanac
    And gobbles all the dates.

A WELL

As round as an apple,
        as deep as a cup,
And all the king's horses
        can't pull it up.

LENGTHENING DAYS

As the days grow longer
The storms grow stronger.

THE TEN O'CLOCK SCHOLAR

    A dillar, a dollar,
    A ten o'clock scholar;
What makes you come so soon?
    You used to come at ten o'clock,
But now you come at noon!

A STAR

Higher than a house,
    higher than a tree.
Oh! whatever can that be?

57

THE LITTLE BIRD

Once I saw a little bird
    Come hop, hop, hop;
So I cried, "Little bird,
    Will you stop, stop,, stop?"

And was going to the window
    To say, "How do you do?"
But he shook his little tail,
    And far away he flew.

BESSY BELL
AND MARY GRAY

Bessy Bell and Mary Gray,
    They were two bonny lasses.
They built their house upon the lea,*
    And covered it with rushes.

Bessy kept the garden gate,
    And Mary kept the pantry.
Bessy always had to wait,
    While Mary lived in plenty.

WINTER

Cold and raw the north winds blow
    Bleak in the morning early.
All the hills are covered with snow,
    And winter's now come fairly.

IF

    If all the world were apple pie,
And all the sea were ink,
And all the trees were bread and
    cheese,
    What should we have to drink?

THE QUARREL

My little old man and I fell out;
I'll tell you what it was all about—
I had money and he had none,
And that's the way the noise begun.

*lea—meadow

Goosey, goosey, gander

Goosey, goosey, gander,
where dost thou wander?
"Upstairs and downstairs
and in my lady's chamber.
There I met an old man
that wouldn't say his prayers,
I took him by his hind legs
and threw him downstairs."

DAFFODILS

Daffy-down-dilly is now come to town
With a petticoat green and bright yellow gown.

A SURE TEST

If you are to be a gentleman,
    And I suppose you'll be,
You'll neither laugh nor smile
    For a tickling of the knee.

ALL THE STARS

On Saturday night I lost my wife,
And where do you think I found her?
    Up in the moon, singing a tune,
    And all the stars around her.

MRS. MASON
BOUGHT A BASIN

Mrs. Mason bought a basin,
Mrs. Tyson said, What a nice 'un.
What did it cost? said Mrs. Frost.
Half a crown, said Mrs. Brown.

Did it indeed? said Mrs. Reed.
It did for certain, said Mrs. Burton.
Then Mrs. Nix up to her tricks
Threw the basin on the bricks.

A GOLDEN APPLE

In marble walls as white as milk,
Lined with a skin as soft as silk,
Within a fountain crystal-clear,
A golden apple doth appear.
No doors there are to this stronghold,
Yet thieves break in and steal the gold.

TO BED, TO BED

"To bed, to bed," says Sleepy-Head.
    "Let's stay awhile," says Slow.
"Put on the pot," says Greedy Sot.
    "We'll sup before we go."

OLD MOTHER HUBBARD

Old Mother Hubbard

Old Mother Hubbard
Went to the cupboard
   To get her poor dog a bone.
But when she came there
The cupboard was bare,
   And so the poor dog had none.

She went to the baker's
   To buy him some bread;
When she came back
   The dog was dead.

She went to the undertaker's
   To buy him a coffin;
When she got back
   The dog was laughing.

She went to the barber's
   To buy him a wig;
When she came back
   He was dancing a jig.

She went to the hatter's
   To buy him a hat;
When she came back
   He was feeding the cat.

She went to the hosier's
   To buy him some hose;
When she came back
   He was dressed in his clothes.

She went to the fruiters
   To buy him some fruit;
When she came back
   He was playing the flute.

She went to the tailor's
   To buy him a coat;
When she came back
   He was riding a goat.

She went to the cobbler's
   To buy him some shoes;
When she came back
   He was reading the news.

The dame made a curtsy,
   The dog made a bow;
The dame said, "Your servant,"
   The dog said, "Bow-wow."

LITTLE TOM TUCKER

Little Tom Tucker
    Sings for his supper.
What shall he eat?
    White bread and butter.
How will he cut it
    Without e'er a knife?
How will he marry
    Without e'er a wife?

JENNY WREN

As little Jenny Wren
    Was sitting by her shed,
She waggled with her tail,
    And nodded with her head.

She waggled with her tail,
    And nodded with her head,
As little Jenny Wren
    Was sitting by the shed.

RAIN

Rain, rain, go away,
    Come again another day;
Little Johnny wants to play.

THE FLYING PIG

Dickery, dickery, dare,
The pig flew up in the air.
The man in brown
    soon brought him down,
Dickery, dickery, dare.

SEE SAW, MARGERY DAW

See saw, Margery Daw,
Jacky shall have a new master:
Jacky must have but a penny a day
Because he can work no faster

OLD KING COLE

Old King Cole
Was a merry old soul,
And a merry old soul was he.
He called for his pipe,
And he called for his bowl,
And he called for his fiddlers three.

Little Jack Jelf

Little Jack Jelf
Was put on the shelf
Because he could not spell "pie."
    When his aunt, Mrs. Grace,
    Saw his sorrowful face,
She could not help saying, "Oh, fie!"

Down by the River

    Down by the river
Where the green grass grows
    Pretty Polly Perkins
    Bleaches her clothes.
    She laughs and she sings,
    And she sings so sweet.
    She calls, Come over,
    Across the street.
He kissed her, he kissed her,
    He took her to town;
    He bought her a ring
    And a damascene* gown.

When I Was a Bachelor

When I was a bachelor
        I lived by myself,
And all the bread and cheese I got
        I put upon a shelf.
The rats and the mice, they made
        such a strife,
I was forced to go to London
        to buy me a wife.
The streets were so broad and
        the lanes were so narrow,
I was forced to bring my wife home
        in a wheelbarrow.
The wheelbarrow broke and
        my wife had a fall,
And down came the wheelbarrow,
        wife and all.

*damascene—patterned

ROBIN AND RICHARD

Robin and Richard
   Were two sleepyheads.
They spend the day
   Just lazing in bed.
Then up starts Robin
   And looks at the sky:
"Oh, brother Richard,
   The sun's very high.
You go before
   With the bottle and bag,
And I will come after
   On little Jack nag."

HOT CODLINS

There was a little woman,
     as I've been told,
Who was not very young,
     nor yet very old.
Now this little woman her living got
By selling codlins,* hot, hot, hot!

THE MULBERRY BUSH

Here we go round the mulberry bush,
The mulberry bush, the mulberry bush,
Here we go round the mulberry bush,
   On a cold and frosty morning.

This is the way we wash our hands,
Wash our hands, wash our hands,
This is the way we wash our hands,
   On a cold and frosty morning.

This is the way we wash our clothes,
Wash our clothes, wash our clothes,
This is the way we wash our clothes,
   On a cold and frosty morning.

This is the way we go to school,
Go to school, go to school,
This is the way we go to school,
   On a cold and frosty morning.

This is the way we come out of school,
Come out of school, come out of school,
This is the way we come out of school,
   On a cold and frosty morning.

* codlins—apples

MARY, MARY

Mary Mary, quite contrary,
How does your garden grow?
With silver bells and cockleshells
And pretty maids all in a row.

HUMPTY DUMPTY

Humpty Dumpty
    Sat on a wall,
Humpty Dumpty
      Had a great fall.

All the king's horses
    And all the king's men
Couldn't put Humpty
      Together again.

HUMPTY DUMPTY

JOHN SMITH

Is John Smith within?—
Yes, that he is.
Can he set a shoe?
Ay, marry, two.
Here a nail and there a nail.
Tick-tack-too.

HANDY-PANDY

Handy-pandy, Jacky dandy,
   Loves plum cake and sugar candy.
He bought some at a grocer's shop,
And please away went hop, hop, hop.

ROUND AND ROUND

Round and round the rugged rock
   The ragged rascal ran.
How many R's are there in that?
   Now tell me if you can.

I SAW A FISHPOND

I saw a fishpond all on fire.
I saw a house bow to a squire.
I saw a parson twelve feet high.
I saw a cottage near the sky.
I saw a balloon made of lead.
I saw a coffin drop down dead.
I saw two sparrows run a race.
I saw two horses making lace.
I saw a girl just like a cat.
I saw a kitten wear a hat.
I saw a man who saw these, too,
   And said, though strange,
      they were all true.

SING, SING

Sing, sing, what shall I sing?
Cat's run away with the
     pudding-string!
Do, do, what shall I do?
The cat has bitten it quite in two.

THE DONKEY

Donkey, donkey, old and gray,
   Open your mouth and gently bray.
Lift your ears and blow your horn,
   To wake the world this sleepy morn.

AS I WAS GOING ALONG

As I was going along, along,
A-singing a comical song, song, song,
The lane that I went was so
      long, long, long,
And the song that I sang was so
      long, long, long,
And so I went singing along.

THIS IS THE WAY

This is the way the ladies ride,
      Prim, prim, prim.
This is the way the gentlemen ride,
      Trim, trim, trim.
Presently come the country folks,
      Hobbledy gee, hobbledy gee.

BELL HORSES

Bell horses, bell horses,[†]
      what time of day?
One o'clock, two o'clock,
      three and away.

LITTLE KING BOGGEN

Little King Boggen he built a fine hall,
Pie-crust and pasty-crust, that was
      the wall;
The windows were made of black
      puddings and white,
And slated* with pancakes—
      you ne'er saw the like!

* slated—roof-tiled
† Refers to the iron horses of town clocks
  that came prancing out on the stroke of the hour.

There were two blackbirds

There were two blackbirds sitting on a hill,
One named Jack, the other named Jill.
Fly away, Jack! Fly away, Jill!
Come again, Jack! Come again, Jill!

Peas-porridge

Peas-porridge hot,
Peas-porridge cold,
Peas-porridge in the pot
Nine days old.
Spell me that in four letters:
I will: T H A T.

PLAY DAYS

How many days has my baby to play?
   Saturday, Sunday, Monday,
   Tuesday, Wednesday, Thursday,
      Friday,
   Saturday, Sunday, Monday.

LEG OVER LEG

Leg over leg,
As the dog went to Dover;
When he came to a stile,
Jump, he went over.

HANNAH BANTRY

Hannah Bantry,
In the pantry,
Gnawing at a mutton bone.
How she gnawed it,
How she clawed it,
When she found herself alone.

FOR BABY

You shall have an apple,
You shall have a plum,
You shall have a rattle,
When papa comes home.

DOCTOR FOSTER

Doctor Foster went to Gloucester
In a shower of rain.
He stepped in a puddle,
Right up to his middle,
And never went there again.

MY MAID MARY

My Maid Mary she minds the dairy,
While I go a-hoeing and mowing
    each morn.
Gaily run the reel and the little
    spinning wheel,
While I am singing and mowing
    my corn.

HIGH DIDDLE DIDDLE

HIGH DIDDLE DIDDLE

High diddle diddle,
The cat and the fiddle,
The cow jumped over the moon.

The little dog laughed
To see such craft,
And the dish ran away with the spoon.

A PIG

As I went to Bonner
  I met a pig
  Without a wig,
Upon my word and honor.

THE WINDS

Mister East gave a feast;
Mister North laid the cloth;
Mister West did his best;
Mister South burnt his mouth
  Eating cold potato.

DAME TROT
AND HER CAT

Dame Trot and her cat
  Led a peaceable life,
When they were not troubled
  With other folks' strife.

When Dame had her dinner
  Pussy would wait,
And was sure to receive
  A nice piece from her plate.

SLEEP, BABY, SLEEP

Sleep, baby, sleep,
Our cottage vale is deep:
The little lamb is on the green,
With woolly fleece so soft and clean—
  Sleep, baby, sleep.

Sleep, baby, sleep,
Down where the woodbines creep;
Be always like the lamb so mild,
A kind and sweet and gentle child.
  Sleep, baby, sleep.

LUCY LOCKET

Lucy Locket lost her pocket,*
Kitty Fisher found it.
There was not a penny in it,
But a ribbon round it.

* pocket—small drawstring purse

THE LION AND THE UNICORN

The lion and the unicorn
Were fighting for the crown.
The lion beat the unicorn
All about the town.
Some gave them white bread,
And some gave them brown;
Some gave them plum-cake,
And sent them out of town.

THE TARTS

The Queen of Hearts,
  She made some tarts
All on a summer's day.
  The Knave of Hearts,
  He stole those tarts,
And took them clean away.

  The King of Hearts
  Called for the tarts,
And beat the Knave full sore.
  The Knave of Hearts
  Brought back the tarts,
And vowed he'd steal no more.

ALPHABET

A was an archer, who shot at a frog.
B was a butcher, and had a great dog.
C was a captain, all covered with lace.
D was a duncehead, and had a red face.
E was an esquire, with pride on his
    brow.
F was a farmer, and followed the plow.
G was a gamester, who had but ill-luck.
H was a hunter, and hunted a buck.
I was an innkeeper, who loved
    to carouse.
J was a joiner, and built up a house.
K was King William, once governed
    this land.
L was a lady, who had a white hand.
M was a miser, and hoarded up gold.
N was a nobleman, gallant and bold.
O was an oyster girl, and went about
    town.
P was a parson, and wore a black gown.
Q was a queen, who wore a silk slip.
R was a robber, and wanted a whip.
S was a sailor, and spent all he got.
T was a tinker, and mended a pot.
U was a usurer,* a miserable elf.
V was a vintner, who drank all himself.
W was a watchman, and guarded the
    door.
X was expensive, and so became poor.
Y was a youth, that did not love school.
Z was a zany, a poor harmless fool.

*usurer—money lender

FIVE TOES

This little piggy went to market,
This little piggy stayed home;
This little piggy had roast beef,
This little piggy had none;
And this little piggy went,
"Wee, wee, wee!"
All the way home.

DARBY AND JOAN

Darby and Joan were dressed in black,
Sword and buckle behind their back.
Foot for foot, and knee for knee,
Turn about Darby's company.

MY PRETTY MAID

"Where are you going, my pretty
    maid?"
"I'm going a-milking, sir," she said.
"May I go with you, my pretty
    maid?"
"You're kindly welcome, sir," she said.
"What is your father, my pretty
    maid?"
"My father's a farmer, sir," she said.
"What is your fortune, my pretty
    maid?"
"My face is my fortune, sir," she said.
"Then I can't marry you, my pretty
    maid."
"Nobody asked you, sir," she said.

JACK SPRAT

Jack Sprat could eat no fat.
His wife could eat no lean;
So 'twixt them both they cleared the cloth,
And licked the platter clean.

WHEN JENNY WREN WAS YOUNG

'Twas once upon a time,
    when Jenny Wren was young,
So daintily she danced
    and so prettily she sung,
Robin Redbreast lost his heart,
    for he was a gallant bird,
So he doffed his hat to Jenny Wren,
    requesting to be heard.

"O, dearest Jenny Wren,
    if you will but be mine,
You shall feed on cherry pie
    and drink new currant wine.
I'll dress you like a goldfinch
    or any peacock gay.
So, dearest Jen, if you'll be mine
    let us appoint the day."

Jenny blushed behind her fan
    and thus declared her mind:
"Since, dearest Bob, I love you well,
    I take your offer kind;
Cherry pie is very nice
    and so is currant wine,
But I must wear my plain brown gown
    and never go too fine."

WHEN JENNY WREN WAS YOUNG

THE BALLOON

What's the news of the day,
Good neighbor, I pray?
They say the balloon
Has gone up to the moon.

SOLOMON GRUNDY

Solomon Grundy,
    Born on Monday,
        Christened on Tuesday,
    Married on Wednesday,
        Took ill on Thursday,
    Worse on Friday,
        Died on Saturday,
    Buried on Sunday.
        This is the end
Of Solomon Grundy.

THREE STRAWS

Three straws on a staff
Would make a baby cry and laugh.

CHRISTMAS

Christmas is coming,
        the goose is getting fat.
Please put a penny in
        the old man's hat.
If you haven't got a penny
        a ha'penny will do;
If you haven't got a ha'penny,
        God bless you.

BONNY LASS

Bonny lass, pretty lass,
    Wilt thou be mine?
Thou shalt not wash dishes
    Nor yet serve the swine.
Thou shalt sit on a cushion
    And sew a fine seam,
And thou shalt eat strawberries,
    Sugar and cream.

DING, DONG, BELL

Ding—dong—bell, the cat's in the well.
  Who put her in?
    Little Johnny Green.
  Who pulled her out?
    Great Johnny Stout.
  What a naughty boy was that
    To try to drown poor pussy cat,
  Who never did him any harm,
  And killed the mice in his
    father's barn.

POLLY AND SUKEY

Polly, put the kettle on,
Polly, put the kettle on,
Polly, put the kettle on,
  We'll all have tea.
Sukey, take it off again,
Sukey, take it off again,
Sukey, take it off again,
  They're all gone away.

ROBIN REDBREAST

Little Robin Redbreast
  sat upon a tree.
Up went Pussy-Cat, down went he.
Down came Pussy-Cat,
  away Robin ran.
Says little Robin Redbreast:
  "Catch me if you can!"

Little Robin Redbreast
  jumped upon a spade.
Pussy-Cat jumped after him,
  and then he was afraid.
Little Robin chirped and sang,
  and what did Pussy say?
Pussy-Cat said: "Mew, mew, mew,"
  and Robin flew away.

THE CROOKED SIXPENCE

There was a crooked man,
And he went a crooked mile,
He found a crooked sixpence
Beside a crooked stile.*
He bought a crooked cat
Which caught a crooked mouse,
And they all lived together
In a little crooked house.

*stile—steps over a wall or fence

I HAD A LITTLE HUSBAND

I had a little husband no bigger than my thumb,
I put him in a pint pot, and there I bid him drum.
I bought a little handkerchief to wipe his little nose,
And a pair of little garters to tie his little hose.

ONE, TWO, BUCKLE MY SHOE

One, two—buckle my shoe.
Three, four—knock at the door.
Five, six—pick up sticks.
Seven, eight—lay them straight.
Nine, ten—a good fat hen.
Eleven, twelve—dig and delve.
Thirteen, fourteen—maids a-courting.
Fifteen, sixteen—maids in the kitchen.
Seventeen, eighteen—maids in waiting;
Nineteen, twenty—my plate's empty.

JACKY, COME GIVE ME YOUR FIDDLE!

"Jacky, come give me your fiddle,
    If ever you mean to thrive."
"Nay, I'll not give my fiddle
    To any man alive.

"If I should give my fiddle
    They'll think that I'm gone mad,
For many a joyful day
    My fiddle and I have had."

THIRTY DAYS HATH SEPTEMBER

Thirty days hath September,
April, June, and November;
February has twenty-eight alone.
All the rest have thirty-one,
Excepting leap-year, that's the time
When February's days
    are twenty-nine.

THE PIPER AND HIS COW

THE PIPER AND HIS COW

There was a piper had a cow,
And he had naught to give her.
He pulled out his pipes and played her a tune,
And bade the cow consider.

The cow considered very well,
And gave the piper a penny,
And bade him play the other tune,
"Corn Rigs Are Bonnie."*

A NEEDLE AND THREAD

Old Mother Twitchett had but one eye,
   And a long tail which she let fly;
And every time
   she went through a gap,
A bit of her tail she left in a trap.

COME OUT TO PLAY

Girls and boys, come out to play,
The moon doth shine as bright as day;
Leave your supper, and leave your
     sleep,
And come with your playfellows
     into the street.
Come with a whoop, come with a call,
Come with a good will or not at all.
Up the ladder and down the wall,
A half-penny roll will serve us all.
You find milk, and I'll find flour,
And we'll have a pudding
     in half an hour.

THE SOW

  The sow came in with the saddle,
  The little pig rocked the cradle,
  The dish jumped up on the table
  To see the pot swallow the ladle.
The spit* that stood behind the door
Threw the pudding-stick on the floor.
  "Odsplut!" said the gridiron,
    "Can't you agree?
  I'm the head constable,
    Bring them to me!"

MARCH WINDS

March winds and April showers
   Bring forth May flowers.

* spit—roasting rod

HARK! HARK!

Hark! Hark!
The dogs do bark,
The beggars are coming to town:
Some in rags,
Some in tags,
And some in velvet gown.

CROSS PATCH

Cross patch, draw the latch,
Sit by the fire and spin.
Take a cup and drink it up,
Then call your neighbors in.

PRIMROSE HILL

As I was going up Primrose Hill,
Primrose Hill was dirty.
There I met a pretty lass,
And she dropped me a curtsey.

Little lass, pretty lass,
Blessings light upon you;
If I had half-a-crown a day,
I'd spend it all upon you.

A DIFFICULT RHYME

What is the rhyme for porringer?
The king he had a daughter fair,
And gave the Prince of Orange her.

I SAW A SHIP A-SAILING

I saw a ship a-sailing,
  A-sailing on the sea;
And, oh! it was all laden
  With pretty things for thee!

There were comfits in the cabin,
  And apples in the hold;
The sails were made of silk,
  And the masts were made of gold.

The four-and-twenty sailors
  That stood between the decks,
Were four-and-twenty white mice
  With chains about their necks.

The captain was a duck,
  With a packet on his back;
And when the ship began to move,
  The captain said, "Quack! Quack!"

HOT BOILED BEANS

Ladies and gentlemen, come to supper—
Hot boiled beans and very good butter.

BAT, BAT

Bat, bat,
Come under my hat,
And I'll give you a slice of bacon.
And when I bake
I'll give you a cake,
If I am not mistaken.

Hot pies

There was an old woman
   Sold puddings and pies;
She went to the mill,
   And dust flew in her eyes.
While through the streets,
To all she meets
   She ever cries:
   "Hot pies—hot pies."

A sunshiny shower

A sunshiny shower
Won't last half an hour.

A swarm of bees

A swarm of bees in May
     Is worth a load of hay.
A swarm of bees in June
     Is worth a silver spoon.
A swarm of bees in July
     Is not worth a fly.

The little mouse

I have seen you, little mouse,
   Running all about the house,
Through the hole your little eye
   In the wainscot* peeping sly,
Hoping soon some crumbs to steal,
To make quite a hearty meal.
Look before you venture out;
See if kitty is about.
If she's gone, you'll quickly run
To the pantry for some fun;
Round about the dishes creep,
Taking into each a peep,
To choose the daintiest that's there,
Spoiling things you do not care.

* wainscot—floor molding

TWO BIRDS

There were two birds sat upon a stone,
Fal de ral-al de ral-laddy.
One flew away and then there was one,
Fal de ral-al de ral-laddy.

The other flew after and then there was none,
Fal de ral-al de ral-laddy.
So the poor stone was left all alone,
Fal de ral-al de ral-laddy.

One of these little birds back again flew,
Fal de ral-al de ral-laddy.
The other came after and then there were two,
Fal de ral-al de ral-laddy.

Says one to the other: "Pray, how do you do?"
Fal de ral-al de ral-laddy.
"Very well, thank you, and pray how are you?"
Fal de ral-al de ral-laddy.

TWO BIRDS

She sells sea-shells*

She sells sea-shells on the sea shore;
The shells that she sells are sea-shells,
    I'm sure.
So if she sells sea-shells on the
    sea shore,
I'm sure that the shells are
    sea-shore shells.

Old woman who lived in a shoe

There was an old woman
    who lived in a shoe,
She had so many children
    she didn't know what to do.
She gave them some broth
    with a slice of brown bread,
Then read them a story
    and sent them to bed.

Jeremiah Obadiah

Jeremiah Obadiah, puff, puff, puff.
When he gives his messages, he
    snuffs, snuffs, snuffs,
When he goes to school by day, he
    roars, roars, roars,
When he goes to bed at night, he
    snores, snores, snores,
When he goes to Christmas treat, he
    eats plum-duff.
Jeremiah Obadiah, puff, puff, puff.

What are little boys made of?

What are little boys made of, made of?
  What are little boys made of?
"Snaps and snails,
    and puppy-dogs' tails;
And that's what little boys
    are made of."

What are little girls made of, made of?
  What are little girls made of?
"Sugar and spice,
    and all that's nice;
And that's what little girls
    are made of."

* This poem is a tongue twister.
  How fast can you say it?

ONE, TWO, THREE, FOUR, FIVE

One, two, three, four, five,
I caught a hare alive.
Six, seven, eight, nine, ten,
I let him go again

THIS IS THE HOUSE THAT JACK BUILT

This is the house that Jack built.

This is the malt
That lay in the house that Jack built.

This is the rat,
That ate the malt*
That lay in the house that Jack built.

This is the cat,
That killed the rat,
That ate the malt
That lay in the house that Jack built.

This is the dog,
That worried the cat,
That killed the rat,
That ate the malt
That lay in the house that Jack built.

This is the cow with the
    crumpled horn,
That tossed the dog,
That worried the cat,
That killed the rat,
That ate the malt
That lay in the house that Jack built.

This is the maiden all forlorn,
That milked the cow with the
    crumpled horn,
That tossed the dog,
That worried the cat,
That killed the rat,
That ate the malt
That lay in the house that Jack built.

This is the man all tattered and torn,
That kissed the maiden all forlorn,
That milked the cow with the
    crumpled horn,
That tossed the dog,
That worried the cat,
That killed the rat,
That ate the malt
That lay in the house that Jack built.

* malt—grain

This is the priest all
  shaven and shorn,
That married the man all
  tattered and torn,
That kissed the maiden all forlorn,
That milked the cow with the
  crumpled horn,
That tossed the dog,
That worried the cat,
That killed the rat,
That ate the malt
That lay in the house that Jack built.

This is the cock that crowed
  in the morn,
That waked the priest all
  shaven and shorn,
That married the man all
  tattered and torn,
That kissed the maiden all forlorn,
That milked the cow with the
  crumpled horn,
That tossed the dog,
That worried the cat,

That killed the rat,
That ate the malt
That lay in the house that Jack built.

This is the farmer sowing his corn,
That kept the cock that
  crowed in the morn,
That waked the priest all
  shaven and shorn,
That married the man all
  tattered and torn,
That kissed the maiden all forlorn,
That milked the cow with the
  crumpled horn,
That tossed the dog,
That worried the cat,
That killed the rat,
That ate the malt
That lay in the house that Jack built.

SHALL WE GO A-SHEARING

"Old woman, old woman, shall we go a-shearing?"
"Speak a little louder, sir, I'm very thick o' hearing."
"Old woman, old woman, shall I kiss you dearly?"
"Thank you, kind sir, I hear very clearly."

DANCE, LITTLE BABY

Dance, little Baby, dance up high!
Never mind, Baby, Mother is by.
Crow and caper, caper and crow,
There, little Baby, there you go!

Up to the ceiling,
      down to the ground,
Backwards and forwards,
      round and round;
Dance, little Baby
      and Mother will sing,
With the merry coral,
      ding, ding, ding!

THE KILKENNY CATS

There were once two cats of Kilkenny.
Each thought there was one cat
      too many;
So they fought and they fit,
And they scratched and they bit,
Till, excepting their nails,
      And the tips of their tails,
Instead of two cats,
      there weren't any.

POOR ROBIN

The north wind doth blow,
   And we shall have snow,
And what will poor robin do then?
      Poor thing!

He'll sit in the barn
   And keep himself warm,
And hide his head under his wing.
      Poor thing!

GOOD KING ARTHUR

GOOD KING ARTHUR

When good King Arthur ruled his land
He was a goodly king;
But he stole three pecks of barley meal
To make a bag-pudding.

A bag-pudding the king did make,
And stuffed it well with plums,
And in it put great lumps of fat
As big as my two thumbs.

The king and queen did eat thereof,
And noblemen beside,
And what they could not eat that night
The queen next morning fried.

GREAT A, LITTLE A

GREAT A, LITTLE A

Great A, little a,
Bouncing B.
The cat's in the cupboard,
And she can't see me.

A

B

C

D

W